D1442198

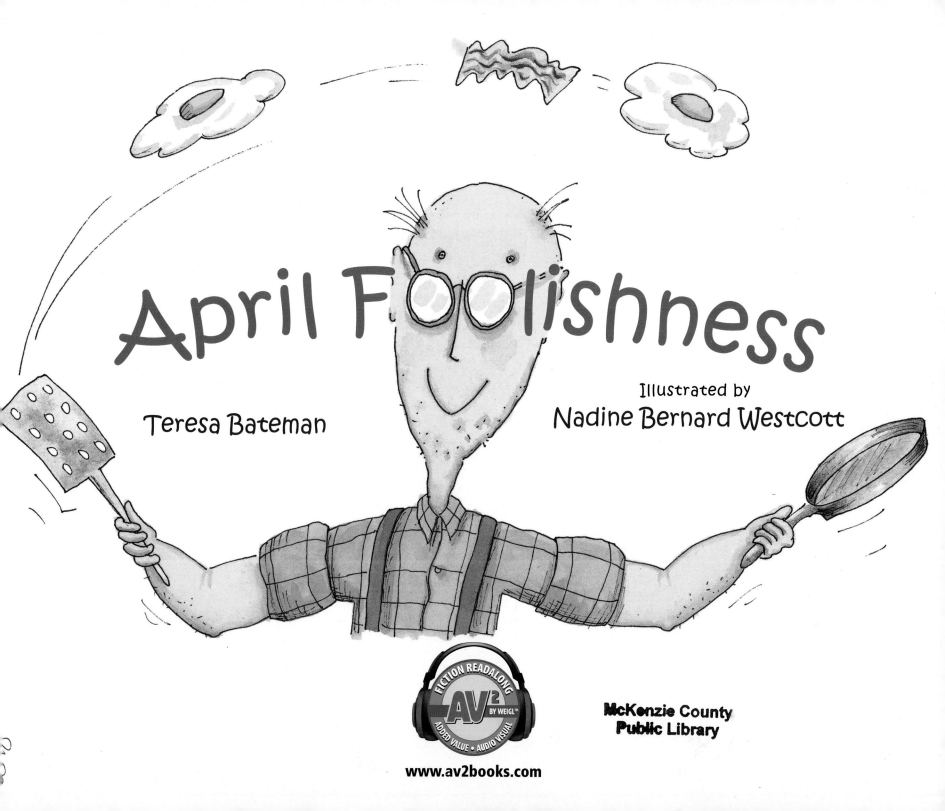

April Foolishness

Teresa Bateman

Illustrated by
Nadine Bernard Westcott

www.av2books.com

Your AV² Media Enhanced book gives you a fiction readalong online. Log on to www.av2books.com and enter the unique book code from this page to use your readalong.

AV² Readalong Navigation

Go to **www.av2books.com**, and enter this book's unique code.

BOOK CODE

W 1 2 1 0 1 3

AV² by Weigl brings you media enhanced books that support active learning.

First Published by

ALBERT WHITMAN & COMPANY
Publishing children's books since 1919

HIGHLIGHTED TEXT

HOME

CLOSE

START READING

TITLE INFORMATION

PAGE TURNING

PAGE PREVIEW

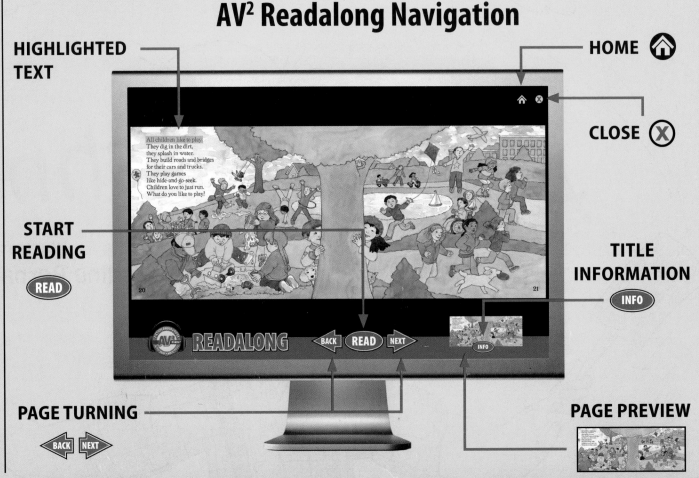

Published by AV² by Weigl
350 5th Avenue, 59th Floor New York, NY 10118
Websites: www.av2books.com   www.weigl.com

Printed in the United States of America in North Mankato, Minnesota
1 2 3 4 5 6 7 8 9 0 18 17 16 15 14

042014
WEP080414

Library of Congress Control Number: 2014937146

ISBN 978-1-4896-2305-8 (hardcover)
ISBN 978-1-4896-2306-5 (single user eBook)
ISBN 978-1-4896-2307-2 (multi-user eBook)

Text copyright ©2004 by Teresa Bateman.
Illustrations copyright ©2004 by Nadine Bernard Westcott.
Published in 2004 by Albert Whitman & Company.

For Suzanne, Jolyn, Shelley Ann, and Rebecca—
can't pull the wool over their eyes!—T.B.

For Oompah and Will—N.B.W.

Life on the farm keeps a gal on her toes.
That's what Grandma thought
as she flung on her clothes.

She grinned, for the grandkids had come for a stay.
And wouldn't you know it—they'd picked the right day!

5

"Grandpa, oh, Grandpa!
The cows have got loose—
I think Big Brown Bessie
just stepped on a goose!"

6

"Imagine," said Grandpa. "Good gracious. Alas!" Then he poured some milk in a tall frosty glass.

They're squawking and squabbling and racing about!"

"Imagine," said Grandpa.
"Amazing. Oh, my!"
as he popped some eggs
into the skillet to fry.

12

"Grandpa, oh, Grandpa! The pigs broke the gate!

13

They're in the tomatoes!
Oh, hurry—don't wait!"

"Imagine," said Grandpa.
"I'm really quite shaken."
He reached in the fridge,
and he got out the bacon.

16

"Grandpa, oh, Grandpa!
The goats are all freed!

They're running around
in a smelly stampede!"

"Imagine," said Grandpa.
"It's really quite scary."
Then he sliced the goat cheese
that he bought from the dairy.

"Grandpa, oh, Grandpa!
The sheep are all gone!

I heard that they're munching on *somebody's* lawn!"

KEEP OFF THE GRASS

Mary had a little lamb

"Imagine," said Grandpa.
"I hope things get better!"
He opened the closet
and got out a sweater.

24

"Grandpa! Oh, why won't you listen to me?
The farm's going nuts. If you'd look, you would see!"

But Grandpa just grinned as he took out the bread
and he popped in some toast for his breakfast, instead.

Then Grandma appeared. "What a hullabaloo!
Who's causing this noise—the grandkids, or you?"

"It's nothing," said Grandpa, "Ignore them, I say.
They're trying to trick me.
It's April Fools' Day!"

26

"But honey," said Grandma, "you'll find, to your sorrow, it's not April Fools' Day today, but tomorrow!"

27

Then Grandpa turned red,
and he gave out a roar.
He sped through the kitchen
and dashed out the door!

Grandma just smiled
as she pulled up a stool.
She nibbled his toast and she called,

"April Fool!"